SuperCat

vs the pesky pirate

Jeanne Willis

Illustrated by Jim Field

HarperCollins *Children's Books*

First published in Great Britain by HarperCollins *Children's Books* 2015
HarperCollins *Children's Books* is a division of HarperCollins*Publishers* Ltd,
HarperCollins Publishers
1 London Bridge Street, London SE1 9GF

Visit us on the web at
www.harpercollins.co.uk

1

SUPERCAT VS THE PESKY PIRATE

Text copyright © Jeanne Willis 2015
Illustrations copyright © Jim Field 2015

Jeanne Willis and Jim Field assert the moral right to be identified
as the author and illustrator of this work.

ISBN: 978-000-751867-8

Printed and bound in England by
Clays Ltd, St Ives plc

MIX
Paper from
responsible sources
FSC® C007454

FSC™ is a non-profit international organisation established to promote
the responsible management of the world's forests. Products carrying the
FSC label are independently certified to assure consumers that they come
from forests that are managed to meet the social, economic and
ecological needs of present and future generations,
and other controlled sources.

Find out more about HarperCollins and the environment at
www.harpercollins.co.uk/green

CONTENTS

Chapter One

ROLL UP, ROLL UP!

"Who wants to go to the funfair today?" said Mrs Jones.

Supercat's paw shot up in the air. He'd read about the fair in the leaflet that had dropped through the letterbox that morning.

It promised to be 'out of this world'!

"Me!" he said, forgetting to behave like the fat, ordinary cat he used to be before he developed superpowers.

James's little sister Mimi gawped at him in amazement.

"Tiger spoke!" she gasped. "He said, 'Me!'"

James glared at her.

"No, he didn't. He was halfway through a miaow and you interrupted him."

It wasn't the first time Mimi had suspected that their pet tabby had hidden talents. Since the day Tiger

had licked a toxic sock he'd found
under James's bed, he had been
blessed with superpowers, just like
Tigerman, the superhero in James's
favourite comic book.

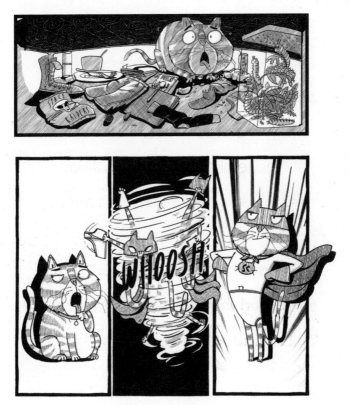

Keen to keep Supercat's secret from his family, James quickly changed the subject. He grabbed the leaflet from his mum and read it out loud to his parents.

"Let Art C. Swackbound take you for a ride at the funfair with a fanfare. Fire-eaters, stilt-walkers, food stalls and a chance to win £1,000,000 in the Lucky Dip!"

"I bet it costs a fortune to get in," said Dad.

Mum shook her head.

"It says here everything's free. Even the rides for the kids."

It sounded almost too good to be true.

"Well, I suppose we could go and check it out," said Dad.

With a cheer, James and Mimi ran upstairs to their rooms to get ready.

"There are *food* stalls – why haven't I been invited?" sighed Supercat as he sat on the bed strumming a sad little tune on the guitar. "*Why, oh why, oh whyyyyyyy…?*"

"You know why," said James fondly. "Cats don't go to funfairs. If you went, it would arouse suspicion."

"Not if I kept my head down," said Supercat. "Hide me in your bag and sneak me in, like the time we went to the zoo."

James thought about it for a second.

12

"Mimi saw you in the car that time. Mum made me take you back home, remember?"

"I'll tuck my tail in this time... I promise!" said Supercat, striking a dramatic chord on the guitar. The strings went ping and snapped.

"*Mi scusi!*" he said, in Italian, waving his arms around and knocking a jar of jellybeans off the shelf.

"I don't know my own strength sometimes."

He might have been as strong as a lion and as fast as a cheetah, but he was still as clumsy as an overgrown kitten. James picked the sticky sweets out of Supercat's fur and opened his backpack.

"Jump in," he said, grinning. "The funfair would be no fun without you."

Supercat did
a triple-flip

and
landed

head-first in the bag with
his bottom in the air.

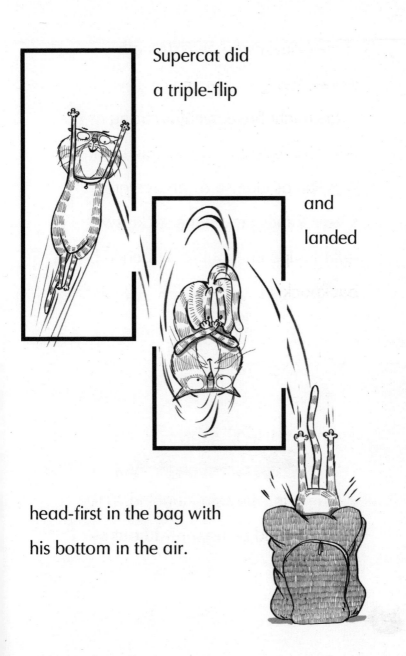

"You won't regret it!" he said.
"Hand me my ultra-stylish superhero
costume! You never know when our
arch-enemy, the mad mathematician,
might turn up."

"You mean Count Backwards?"
said James. "I doubt we'll see that evil
villain again. Not after you ejected
him from the president's plane in our
last adventure."

"Even so, I'd hate to be caught with
my pants down," said Supercat.

James rummaged under the bed
and found the costume Supercat had
made from Mimi's leotard and Dad's

16

old Y-fronts. He tried not to giggle. It looked even funnier on than off, but rather than upset him, James passed it solemnly to Supercat. Then he zipped up the backpack and slung it over his shoulders as he made his way downstairs.

It was only a short walk to the fair but James's backpack soon began to wriggle like mad. James lagged behind in case Mimi saw and started asking awkward questions. Luckily, she seemed to be far too busy watching the clowns, the unicyclists and the jugglers parading along the street to take any notice.

"Are you all right in there, Supercat?" whispered James. "Can you breathe?"

James undid the flap. To his surprise, Supercat had his pants on his

head and was peering through the leg holes.

"What's so funny?" said Supercat. "Have I got gravy on my whiskers again?"

James gave the pants' elastic a gentle ping.

"Your costume's on upside down."

"*Zut alors!*" exclaimed Supercat in his best French, struggling to get his legs out of his leotard sleeves. "That's the last time I get ready without a long mirror..."

Just then a strange figure in a mask and top hat walked past. His suit and hat were half black and half white and he had a flute in his top pocket.

"I see I'm not the only one who got dressed in the dark," chortled Supercat.

"Roll up, roll up!" roared the man, patting Mimi on the head. "Welcome to the fairest funfair on earth! Free rides for every child! Free food and drink for every parent!"

"That must be Mr Swackbound," said James. "What a lovely, generous man."

"It just goes to show you should never judge someone by his outfit," said Supercat, ducking his head down as Mum came over.

"Mimi needs the toilet," Mum said, shouting over the fairground din. "Do you need to go, James?"

A group of kids standing nearby that James knew from school laughed. He cringed with embarrassment.

"No, I'm going on the ghost train," he said, trying to sound tough.

"OK," Mum said. "Meet us by the Lucky Dip in half an hour. Dad's determined to win a million."

James marched off, avoiding eye contact with the sniggering kids. He was furious with his mother for showing him up like that.

"I'm ten!" he hissed as he climbed into the front carriage of the ghost train. "Why does she have to treat me like a baby in front of everyone? If she knew I was a crime fighter, she might show me a bit more respect."

"Alas, she can never know," said Supercat. "But *I* know and that is all that matters, my friend. Meanwhile, I am bursting to get out of this bag."

"Why, do you need a wee too?" said James.

Supercat gave him a hard stare. "Sometimes, James, you are so like your mother."

James smiled. It was impossible to stay in a sulky mood at Art C. Swackbound's funfair. It was far too exciting, with all the bright lights, the sound of the merry-go-round and the smell of candy floss. And now at last the ghost train was beginning to move, rattling along the rickety tracks

as it headed towards a dark tunnel
ahead. James took his backpack off
and helped Supercat into the seat
next to him, strapping him in.

"Don't be scared," said James as a
cackling witch swung past on a broom.

"Scared... *moi?*" said Supercat indignantly. "There is nothing to fear. My super-feline night vision tells me that these spooks and spiders are no more real than that hideous zombie lurching toward— *aghhhhhhhh!*"

25

Supercat let out a piercing caterwaul.
James almost shot out of his seat.

"W-what's up?" he stammered. "It's
not a real zombie... is it?"

"It's far worse than that," said
Supercat. "Look at his shoes!"

James could hardly believe his ears.

"Who are you, the Fashion Police? What's wrong with his shoes?"

Supercat pointed wildly at the zombie's boots and whispered something behind his paw.

"They've got numbers on them?" repeated James.

James squinted at the footwear in the gloomy headlights of the train and his jaw dropped open. Sure enough, the shoes were covered in sums. His heart began to pound. That was no zombie – that was a member of Count Backwards's deadly Calculator Crew! But what was he doing on a fairground ride?

"Something is afoot!" said Supercat. "And it smells like..."

"Cheese?" said James.

"No," said Supercat, narrowing his eyes. "Trouble!"

Chapter Two

TOOT, TOOT

"Art C Swackbound…" muttered James as the ghost train did another circuit. "Now I think of it, that name does sound strangely familiar."

He rearranged all the letters in his

head to try and make a new name:

A-R-T C. S-W-A-C-K-B-O-U-N-D…

B-U-R-T C-A-N-D-A-W-O-C-K-S?

D-R. S-T-A-N W. B-O-U-C-A-C-K?

As the ghost train thundered towards the light at the end of the tunnel, it suddenly came to him.

"C-O-U-N-T B-A-C-K-W-A-R-D-S! It's him again!" James cried.

"Who again?" said Supercat.

"Swackbound is really Backwards," said James.

Supercat looked puzzled.

"He seemed quite intelligent to me," he said.

"I meant Backwards as in *Count* Backwards!" said James. "Quick, get back in my bag. We need to find out what his game is."

"*Mamma mia!*" exclaimed Supercat in Italian. "Yes, we do! And I bet it's not 'Hook the Duck'."

As soon as the train stopped, James leapt out of the carriage. Blinking in the sunlight, he noticed that the man in charge of the ride was also wearing shoes with sums on. So were the men who ran the helter-skelter, the rifle range and the swing boats.

"I don't believe it!" puffed James.

"Even the candyfloss man is a
Calculator!"

"Any sign of the Count?" called
Supercat from inside the backpack.

James searched the crowd for the man in the weird black and white suit and top hat, but there was no sign of him.

"Let's go on the Big Wheel," James said. "It'll be the best place to spot him from."

There were two miserable-looking clowns with big red noses in charge of the Big Wheel – a short, fat one and a tall, thin one. They were wearing such enormous clowns' shoes that the numbers on them were plain to see.

Even in disguise, James recognised

33

them straight away – they were the Count's head henchmen, Mr Plus and Mr Minus! He and Supercat had done battle with them before, but now wasn't the time to confront them. He pulled his hood over his head and zipped up his jacket to his nose so they wouldn't recognise him.

"I hate little children, don't you, Mr Plus?" said Mr Minus.

The fat one smiled horribly at James and ushered him on to the ride.

"With all my heart, Mr Minus," said Mr Plus. "But not as much as the Count does!"

Mr Plus clanged the safety bar
shut over James's lap, and when the
ride was fully loaded with children
he pressed the starter button. The Big

Wheel began to turn. As soon as they were up in the air where no one could see them, Supercat scrabbled out of the bag and sat next to James.

"Look!" he cried, pointing into the distance. "Over there!"

"Have you spotted Count Backwards?" said James.

"No, the Fish and Chip shop!" said Supercat. "It's amazing what you can see from up here, isn't it?"

James sighed. "You're supposed to be using your super-feline vision to find the enemy."

Supercat shielded his eyes and

scanned the horizon.

"You mean the vet?" he said. "He's definitely my enemy. The last time I saw him, he stuck his thermometer right up my... why have we stopped?"

Just as they reached the top, the Big Wheel came to a shuddering halt.

"Maybe a kid threw up and they're letting him off," said James. "I wonder why no grown-ups are allowed on any of the rides?" he said, noticing a sign at the entrance. "It seems a bit odd."

Supercat twiddled his thumbs. He'd never had thumbs when he was an ordinary cat and he still hadn't got over the novelty.

"I expect it'll start up in a minute," he said. "Once they've wiped the seat."

They sat there patiently for a while, swinging in mid-air. James checked his watch.

"We've been stuck here for ten minutes," he said. "Maybe there's a mechanical fault, and the wheel won't go forwards."

"Or maybe it's Backwards!" said Supercat.

"I don't mind if it goes backwards

38

or forwards, as long as it goes," said James.

"No, I mean maybe it's Count Backwards!" said Supercat, standing on his chair, his hero cape blowing in the wind. "I don't know if you've noticed, but ours isn't the only ride that has stopped."

James looked down. It was true. The Aeroplane Chairs were suspended in the air, the rollercoaster had come to a halt on the highest loop and the horses on the merry-go-round had frozen in mid-leap – none of the children could get off!

James felt a shiver run down his spine.

"We're all trapped!" he said. "It must be a deliberate act of vandalism."

The organ had stopped playing.
The fairground men had stopped
calling. For a moment, there was
an eerie silence. Supercat's ears
swivelled like fuzzy windmills.

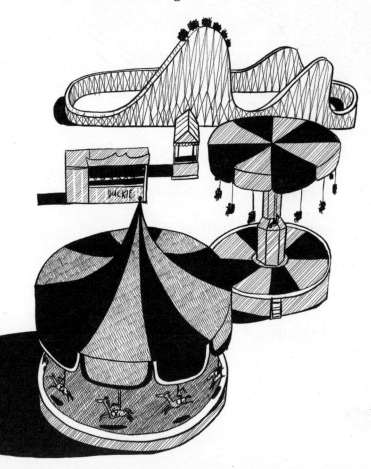

"I don't like the sound of this," he muttered, thrashing his tail.

James couldn't hear a thing.

"The sound of what?"

"A terrible twit in a two-toned suit tooting a flute," said Supercat, teetering dangerously on the edge of his seat. "Look – there he is, the pesky pied parper!"

"Who?" said James, confused.

"Count Backwards! He's playing some sort of instrument and all the grown-ups are following him."

James clung to the edge of his seat and looked over. Down below, there was a long line of adults dancing behind Count Backwards. As the Count skipped along like a maniac, blowing his flute, more and more grown-ups joined the growing conga line behind him.

"Why would they all abandon their kids just to hear him play?" wondered James.

"Search me," said Supercat. "It's hardly a catchy tune. And it gets worse."

"What, the tune?" asked James.

"No, the situation," said Supercat. "Look – your parents are at the front of the queue!"

"What?"

By now, James was completely baffled.

"But they hate folk music. They'd have to be hypnotised to enjoy it."

"They do seem to be in a trance from where I'm standing," said Supercat.

"That's it!" James shouted. "Count Backwards has hypnotised everyone with his loony tune. He's kidnapping all the grown-ups – including Mum and Dad!"

"And Mimi," added Supercat, pointing.

James paused for a second. His interfering little sister was being kidnapped?

"It's not all bad then," he said. "But why just Mimi? Why not the other kids?"

Then he remembered – she was in the loo when the rides started!

By now, all the kids stranded on the rides were crying for their mummies and daddies. But nobody could hear their screams. Count Backwards had lured every single grown-up at the funfair away from their children, and he seemed to be leading them into the Bouncy Castle along with his Calculator Crew.

"We have to get off this Big Wheel," said James. "But I can't think how."

"I can," said Supercat grandly. "We climb!"

James's stomach lurched. He was no coward, but he didn't have a great head for heights. He grabbed Supercat by the tail.

"*Please* sit down!" he wailed. "I need you alive or Count Backwards will get away!"

Supercat patted his hand with his paw.

"Look, Tigerman didn't defeat villains by sitting down. But worry not! When I said 'we' I meant me. Tiger Power, rargh, rargh, rargh!"

And to James's horror, Supercat flung himself over the edge of the seat and dangled from the safety bar like a stripy trapeze artist. The ground was a hundred feet below.

But there was no safety net.

Chapter Three
All Aboard

"Hang on tight!" yelled James.
"And whatever you do, don't
look down."

He could hardly bear to watch
as Supercat swung backwards and
forwards in mid-air, trying to feel for

the nearest spoke on the Big Wheel.

"You nearly had it then," said

James. "Bit to your left…"

"Right," said Supercat.

"No, *left*!" cried James.

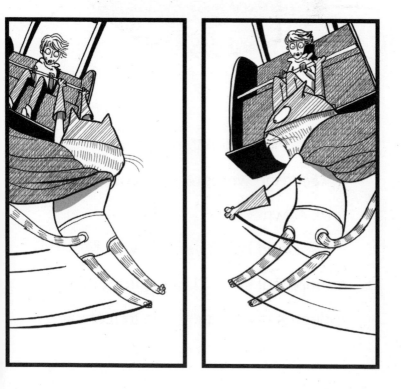

Supercat swung towards it
and hooked it with his back feet.
Suddenly, he let go of the safety bar
with his thumbs.

"Noooo!!" cried James.

He squeezed his eyes shut. Not
even Supercat could survive a fall
from that height... surely? It was only
when he heard singing that he dared
to open his eyes again.

*"He flies through the air with the
furriest knees,*

*"The daring young cat on the flying
trapeze!"*

Supercat was upside down, clinging

to the spoke by his toes with his cloak wrapped round him like a fat fruit bat.

"Are you stuck?" called James.

"No, I'm just hanging around," said Supercat. "Planning my next move!"

He swung his tail backwards and forwards like a pendulum. Just as it looked as if he was about to lose his grip, he folded himself in half, reached between his tabby ankles and grabbed the spoke. James clapped and cheered.

"Hooray! I was afraid I was going to lose you."

"I was afraid I was going to lose my breakfast," confessed Supercat. "But luckily for the people below, I'm glad to report my Meatybix stayed put."

Humming the theme tune from his

favourite cat food advert, he inched his way towards the wheel hub until he looked no bigger than a spider on a giant steel web. James sat back and prayed that Supercat would get down in one piece.

A few moments later, there was a surge of electricity followed by a metallic clanking sound, and the Big Wheel began to turn again.

Wow! Supercat must have got down in record time and started the wheel, thought James. But then he heard organ music coming from the merry-go-round too. By the time his

seat had reached ground level, he
realised that all the rides had started
up again. He threw off the safety bar,
jumped out and looked
around for his
partner in crime-
fighting.

"Never fear,
Supercat is here!"
yelled a familiar voice.

James looked up as
Supercat slid down the leg of the
Big Wheel like a feline fireman on
a pole. He landed with a bump
at James's feet and looked up at
him in astonishment.

"*Sacre Bleu!*" he exclaimed in French. "How did you get down?"

"The wheel started up again all by itself," said James.

Supercat's face pleated into a frown. "Did it?" He'd been too busy clinging on to notice.

"I don't know why I bother sometimes," he sighed.

"Because you're a superhero who's determined to rid the world of evil," said James. "Why would the Count make the rides stop like that, and then start again? It's almost like he wanted all the children out of the way for a while."

"But why?" asked Supercat.

"I don't know, but if we hurry, we might still be able to stop him. Head for the Bouncy Castle!"

Supercat straightened his mask and dusted himself down, and the two of them raced across the fairground, dodging between the crowds of

wailing kids who were looking for
their parents.

"Wait for me!" puffed James.

Supercat was running so fast, the
grass had caught fire. He wasn't
going to let the Count get away from
him this time.

"There he goes, the tooting, fluting
fool!" he snarled, shooting past
the beer tent as Backwards led the

last hypnotised grown-ups into the Bouncy Castle. Supercat pumped his paws and went even faster.

"Mind you don't trip over that guy rope..." yelled James.

Too late! Supercat caught his foot,

catapulted into the air…

and landed face-down in an undignified heap. He lay there without moving. James felt his pulse.

"Are you all right, Supercat? Speak to me!"

"I've gone blind," he wailed.

"Your cloak just fell over your head," said James, whisking it back. "What can you see now?"

Supercat sat up and narrowed his eyes.

"I see that Count Backwards is even more evil than we thought. My super-vision tells me that he didn't take his shoes off before he got on the Bouncy Castle!"

"It's hardly the crime of the century," said James.

Supercat stroked his chin, deep in thought.

"Ah, but the fact that he *didn't* strip to his socks tells me that this Bouncy Castle is not what it seems, my friend!"

As if to prove him right, an engine started up inside the castle. There was a loud **ker-lunk** and a set of wheels dropped down from beneath it.

"It's Count Backwards's motorcastle!" groaned James.

As he spoke, the motorcastle did a three-point turn and, going from nought to sixty in five seconds, it raced past the donkey rides and out of the funfair gates.

"It's heading for the main road!"
said James. "We'll never catch it on
foot, not even at super-speed."

Supercat almost pulled his whiskers
out in despair.

"If only you'd brought your bike," he said. "I could have used pedal power."

James looked around in despair. "Look, grab that clown's unicycle!" he said.

Supercat thought it was a joke.

"I hate to point this out," he laughed, "but it only has one wheel."

"It's better than no wheels," insisted James. "Hold it steady. I'll steer, you sit on the saddle in front of me and pedal."

Supercat did as he was told, but even with superpowers, it wasn't easy riding a unicycle. First he crashed into the chemical toilet.

THUD!

Then he reversed into the hoopla stand.

But he soon got the hang of it and a moment later they were speeding across the field at breakneck speed with James hanging on to the handlebars for dear life.

"Can you see the motorcastle yet?" he yelled.

"It's just gone over the hill. It's heading for the docks!" said Supercat. "Any minute now, you should be able to see it with your normal vision."

But he spoke too soon.

"Why are you hissing?" said James.

"I was going to ask you the same question," panted Supercat.

"I'm *not* hissing," said James.

Supercat's ears swivelled to attention.

"If you're not hissing… and I'm not… it must be… the bike!"

"Oh no…" wailed James.

They jumped off and examined the tyre. It was as flat as a cowpat.

"Oh poo… dles," swore Supercat.

Looking in the saddle bag, James found a repair kit.

"Quick – I'll patch it, you pump it!" said James.

"There's no pump," said Supercat. "I'll have to use my super-puff to blow it up."

A minute later and the bike was
fixed, but there wasn't another
moment to lose. They climbed back
on and hurried down to the docks at
the speed of light.

"I can see them! Oh no, we're too
late!" said James, as they screeched to
a halt on the jetty. Count Backwards
had already piped all the grown-ups

out of the motorcastle and up the gangway on to a strange-looking ship.

"All aboard the *Dawn Crockabust*!" boomed Count Backwards. "What a 5-4-3-2-wonderful day for a mystery cruise."

James looked at the name on the ship.

"D-A-W-N C-R-O-C-K-A-B-U-S-T?" he said angrily. "I might have known. Shift those letters around and guess what else they spell?"

Supercat wasn't great at anagrams, but he was learning.

"A C-R-A-B S-T-U-CK D-O-W-N?" he said.

"C-O-U-N-T B-A-C-K-W-A-R-D-S!" said James.

"Of course!" groaned Supercat. "But this is no time for word games! We must get on board and stop the

count before he runs away to sea
with your family."

Just then they heard a loud
clanging sound and a shout.

"Anchors away, me hoodwinked
hearties!" cried the Count.

It was too late – the ship had
already sailed.

Chapter Four
Yo, Ho, Ho!

"**W**e can't let Count Backwards rule the waves!" said Supercat, throwing off his cape and stripping down to his fur.

"What are you doing?" said James.

"I'm going to swim after that ship!"

74

Supercat announced. He eased
himself down on to the
side of the jetty and
dipped his toe in the
sea. "Brrr... chilly!"

"You can't
doggy-paddle all
that way, can
you?" said James.

Supercat
screwed up his face in disgust.

"*Doggy?* How many times have I
asked you not to use the 'D' word?"

Whatever he wanted to call it,
there was no way James was letting

Supercat go without him – even Supercat couldn't defeat the Count alone. And although Supercat could swim like a tiger, James only had his twenty-five-metre swimming certificate and a big hole in his underpants.

"Put your costume back on, Supercat," he said. "We're a team – we stick together. We'll have to sail after them!"

James had just wandered off round the harbour to find a spare yacht when he heard Supercat's call.

"Yoo hoo, Pedilooo!"

James looked over to where

Supercat was pointing, below the sea wall. There was a paddle boat bobbing about in the water, moored with a rope.

"Great! Jump in, Supercat," said James. "You pedal, I'll navigate."

Supercat tutted loudly and folded his arms. "How come you always get to navigate?"

"Because you're the one with superpowers," James reminded him as he clambered into the boat. "If I pedal, Count Backwards will have sailed over the horizon by the time we get there."

"Over my dead body!" said Supercat, leaping into the seat of the pedalo. With his eye fixed on the *Dawn Crockabust*, his knees went into overdrive.

"Thar she blows!" he yelled, his paws pumping on the pedals like pistons. "Splice the mainbrace! Heave-ho!"

"I never knew you could speak Pirate," said James as the pedalo cut through the waves.

"Ooh, arr!" said Supercat. "My grandfather was a ship's cat, you know. Look, we're gaining on her! Prepare to board the enemy vessel!"

With a nifty bit of reverse-pedalling, Supercat drew the pedalo alongside the Count's ship. He tied it fast with a sailor's knot, sprang on to the rope ladder and, holding out his paw, pulled James up on to the rungs.

"It's Backwards or me this time!" Supercat bellowed, swinging up the ladder like a monkey.

"Shhh!" panicked James. "We need to use the element of surprise."

"The elephant of surprise?" said Supercat. "Speak up, I can't hear you, even with my super-hearing. It's really windy."

"We need to sneak on and stow away!" shouted James over the shrieking gale.

"Shhh!" yelled Supercat. "The Count will hear us!"

They climbed to the top of the ladder in silence and looked down into the ship. It was manned by a motley crew of pirates, all with numbers on their boots.

"Yo ho ho and a bottle of rum, Mr Minus?" said Mr Plus.

"The sun is over the yardarm. Rip the cork out, Mr Plus," said Mr Minus.

Supercat gritted his fangs.

"Calculator Crew!" he spat.

They waited until Mr Plus and Mr Minus weren't looking and climbed on board, hiding themselves behind a row of barrels.

"Can you see Mum, Dad and Mimi?" whispered James, peeking out from behind a barrel.

But there was no sign of them, or any of the grown-ups.

"Maybe they're in the poop cabin," said James.

"Let's go there. I need the toilet," said Supercat, hopping up and down.

"The poop cabin isn't a toilet," said James, laughing. "It's the raised deck at the back where the helmsman navigates."

Supercat's face fell.

"So where can I poop? It's urgent!"

"As urgent as finding Count Backwards?" said James.

Supercat lifted his leg and squeezed

 out a squeaky little fart.

"Sorted," he said. "False alarm. I told you it was windy. Now I can concentrate on finding your folks and that foul, flute-tooting fiend. Lead on, James!"

They sidled along the ship's side towards the stern, steering clear of the Calculators, but the parents and the Count were still nowhere to be seen.

"You'd think he'd be easy to

spot in his crazy suit and hat," said Supercat.

James shrugged. "Maybe he's changed."

Supercat put a fatherly arm round him.

"Bless you," he said. "Always thinking the best of everyone. But people never change. Once a villain, always a villain."

"I meant, maybe he's changed into a pirate's outfit," said James. "Hang on a sec... Who is that strange figure standing by the ship's wheel?"

Supercat craned his neck to get a

better look at the man.

"Let me see. Breeches... tricorn hat... cutlass.... looks like a pirate to me!"

That moment a gust of wind whipped up and snatched the pirate's hat away, revealing a mop of mad, white hair.

"5-4-3-2-windy!" cried the Count, waving his cutlass in the air.

"Count Backwards!" whispered James.

But before they had a chance to go after him, Count Backwards sounded the foghorn five times, opened a

hatch and threw himself below deck.
He was followed by a steady stream
of Calculators, pushing and shoving
each other in a great hurry to jump in
after him. Once below, they battened
down the hatch.

James and Supercat were alone on the deck. There was an eerie creaking sound, then suddenly the sails lowered all by themselves, the rigging unravelled and the masts folded down like telescopes.

"I've got a horrible sinking feeling..." said Supercat.

"That's because we're sinking!" said James.

A glass roof rolled up and over the top of the deck and sealed them in like figurines in a snow shaker. The waves crashed over the top.

"We're going down with the ship!"
wailed Supercat.

But this was no ordinary ship. The
Dawn Crockabust had morphed...
into a submarine!

"We're going to drown! Quick, get
in the poop..." said James.

"I'm afraid we're already in it,"
said Supercat.

Chapter Five

DRACK
SCUBATOWN

"Incredible!" said James as they sank deeper into the ocean. "I hate to say it, but making a ship that turns into a submarine? The Count's a genius."

Supercat peered out of the poop

cabin and licked his lips as a shoal of delicious-looking pilchards swam over the glass roof.

"Hmm?" he drooled.

"I was just thinking, it's a shame Backwards went mad," said James. "If he hadn't, the Secret Service would never have fired him. He could have used his genius for the good, instead of kidnapping my parents. Why would he want them, anyway?"

"Maybe he's an orphan," said Supercat.

"So why kidnap the other adults?" said James. "Two parents are enough for anyone. And why take them to the bottom of the ocean? They can't live there."

"Can't they?" said Supercat, pressing his nose to the glass. "Look!"

As the submarine passed through a curtain of seaweed, James spotted hundreds of bright lights in the distance, as if a whole city had left its lamps on.

Then he realised what he was seeing.

"It *is* a city!" he gasped.

He could see it quite clearly now— a huge underwater world, all built under a massive, waterproof glass igloo with an entry tunnel at one end.

"People live here," James murmured. "What *is* this place?"

By the entrance to the tunnel they could see a hexagonal clock tower, with only certain hours displayed on the clock's face – 5, 4, 3, 2 and 1 – and to confirm their worst fears, there was a large neon sign fixed to it…

"D-R-A-C-K S-C-U-B-A-T-O-W-N…" read Supercat. "Is that an anagram for You-Know-Who?"

James jiggled round the letters in his head.

"C-O-U-N-T B-A-C-K-W-A-R-D-S!

I'm afraid so. What I don't understand is..."

But before he could finish his sentence, the circular door at one end of the entry tunnel twisted open. The submarine cruised into the tunnel and docked.

"Why aren't we moving?" said Supercat.

"There's a red traffic light," said James. "I think we're being held while the water drains out of the tunnel."

The submarine waited while the door behind it twisted shut again, sealing out the sea, and the water in the tunnel flushed away beneath them, as if someone had pulled a toilet chain.

The traffic light turned amber.

"I really need a tiddle," said Supercat.

"Hold on," said James. "The lights are changing."

"I'll need changing if I have to hold on much longer," winced Supercat.

At last the traffic light turned green, the revolving door in front of them that led to the city slid open. There was a loud whoosh and a clunk as the escape hatch on the submarine opened and a ramp dropped down.

Supercat's ears began to swivel.

"Fol-dee roll... fiddle-dee-dee...
Count Backwards, the pied parper,
is at it again!" he said, as the Count
danced down the ramp. He was back
in his top hat and suit, tooting his
flute. Unable to resist, the hypnotised
grown-ups followed him out of the
submarine, through the city doors
and were led like lambs into a fleet of
waiting taxis.

"Follow those cabs!" said Supercat,
dashing out of the poop cabin.

James held him back.

"Wait until the Calculators get off," he said. "If they catch us, we're stuffed."

"I'll fight them," said Supercat, slicing the air with his paws. "I have a black belt in Salami, the ancient sport of Egyptian kings."

"I remember," said James. "You're extraordinary. But we're outnumbered."

Supercat paced up and down.

"If we don't hurry, the door to the city will shut," he said. "If it's strong enough to hold back the sea, I'm not sure I can open it, even with my super paws."

James thought quickly.

"OK, we go below. We creep out of the escape hatch. Then when the last of the Calculators enters through the revolving door, we sneak into the section behind and squat down."

"Then what?" said Supercat.

"Then they walk off, and we go in the opposite direction."

It sounded so simple. But Supercat

99

had never been through a revolving door before. By the time he'd stopped going round and round as if he was on the Whirlitzer at Swackbound's funfair, the Calculators – and the cabs – were miles away.

"Why didn't you get out when I said?" asked James, as Supercat staggered off.

"Dizzy," said Supercat, trying not to fall over.

James steadied him. They stood still for a moment and drank in the view. It was like being in a gigantic fish bowl, only with the water and the fish on the outside. A shark swam past the city wall and glared at Supercat.

"I hope the glass doesn't break," he shuddered.

To his surprise, James laughed out loud.

"You won't find it so funny if a shark gets in," said Supercat.

"I was laughing at that building," said James, pointing to a public toilet nearby; it was shaped like a number two. Supercat nipped into the Gents and returned a few minutes later, looking very relieved.

"You have bog roll stuck to your foot," said James.

"Ugh," said Supercat. "It's covered in sums."

And it wasn't just the toilet paper that had a mathematical theme. As they walked through the city, they soon noticed that everything was designed with numbers in mind. The rooftops were tiled like graph paper. The bingo hall was shaped like a huge bingo ball. The streets were paved with dominoes and the kerbs were painted like tape measures. Even the dance school had numbered ballet positions carved into the brickwork – 1st position, 2nd position, 3rd...

"I never knew Backwards was into
ballet," said James.

"He's certainly leading us a merry
dance," replied Supercat.

As they turned the corner into Algebra Road, they came across a busy market. There were several stalls, selling everything from diving suits to sausages. While the man in charge of the diving stall was busy at the till, Supercat tried on some flippers and a snorkel and pretended to swim.

"James! I'm a catfish... James?"

But James was busy talking to the cheesemonger, the fishmonger, the greengrocer, anyone who would listen – had they seen his mum and dad? He described them as best he could, but no one had seen them, or a bratty little girl with pigtails.

"Try the main square in the city centre," said the cake seller, wiping her hands on her apron that was printed with the twelve-times table. "Go left at Right Angle Road, right at Left Angle Lane then forty-five degrees north of the hypotenuse. You can't miss it."

"There's a *hypotenuse*?" said Supercat, looking nervously over his shoulder. "I don't fancy bumping into him. They kill more people in Africa than crocodiles, you know."

"That's a hippopotamus," said James. "A hypotenuse is the longest side of a right-angled triangle."

"Even so, you can't be too careful," said Supercat, striding off. "Now, did she say to go right at Left Angle Road or Left at Right Angle Lane?"

"We're not lost, are we?" said James as they went past a statue of a protractor for the third time.

"No," fibbed Supercat. "We're taking the scenic route."

He didn't want to worry James, but being underwater in an air-conditioned glass bubble was playing havoc with his catnav.

"That's it! *Air*-conditioning!" he said.

"What about it?" said James.

Supercat held up his paw for silence, his ears swivelling manically as he listened.

"My super-feline hearing tells me there's a huge air-conditioning unit based in this direction," he said, pointing. "If we follow that sound, it should lead us to the city centre!"

"You're a genius. Where would I

be without you?" said James, running after him.

Left down Equal Road, right down Decimal Drive, through Parallel Alley and suddenly they found themselves in a large central square. James looked at the road sign.

"We're in Set Square. This must be it!" he said.

At the far side of the square there was a huge crystal castle.

"I wonder who lives there?" said Supercat.

James looked at the numbers on the front door.

"I'll give you 5-4-3-2-one guess," he said.

Supercat peered through the letterbox.

109

"No sign of Backwards in the hall," he said. "I'll boot the door open."

James felt under the mat.

"Let's use this key. You don't want glass in your paws."

He turned it in the lock and they tiptoed inside.

Chapter Six

DO THE
MATHS

James and Supercat crept along the castle hallway and into a room full of pumping machines and metal tubes. In the middle, there was an operating desk covered in buttons and dials. One was labelled 'air-conditioning' and another 'temperature gauge'.

"I wonder what this red switch does?" said Supercat, giving it a flick.

Drack Scubatown was plunged into darkness.

"It must control the city's electrics. You've switched all the lights off!" said James. Supercat snapped them back on.

"Thank goodness!" said a voice from upstairs. "I can see what I'm doing now. Drop your trousers and don't be such a baby."

James's mouth fell open.

"That's Mum's voice!" he said.

They charged up the stairs, falling over each other to rescue her. Supercat got to the landing first and put his ear to the nearest door. Behind it, someone was yelling "ooch" and "ouch" in a high-pitched voice – was Mum in mortal danger? He looked through the keyhole and gulped at the hideous sight before him.

"What's going on?" said James.

Supercat put his paws over his eyes.

"You don't want to know."

"Let me see, it can't be that bad," said James.

But it was worse. Standing in front of an aquarium the length of the bedroom was his mother. She had Count Backwards in a headlock with his trousers round his ankles and was waving a pair of tweezers at him.

"Fancy sitting on your own pet sea urchin!" she scolded. "I'll never get the spines out if you keep fidgeting!"

"But it *hurts*, Mummy," moaned the Count.

James had heard enough.

"She's not your mum, she's mine!" he said, storming into the room.

Count Backwards looked at him wearily and slapped himself on the forehead.

"*You* again?" he groaned, pulling his trousers up. "Go away. She's my mummy now."

"No, she isn't!" said James. "Mum,

115

tell him!"

His mother looked James up and down blankly.

"Sorry, dear... have we met?"

"I'm your *son*!" insisted James.

The Count adjusted his braces and waltzed over to his black and white suit jacket, which was hanging over a set of golf clubs by his teddy collection. He felt in the pockets and pulled out his flute.

"I made her forget who you are," he sniggered, dancing a mad little hornpipe. He turned to James's mother and tugged her hand like a toddler. "*I'm* your blue-eyed boy now, aren't I, Mummy?" he simpered. "Go and make my dinner. I want fish fingers but no peas... I *hate* peas."

"Very well, son," she said, shuffling off to prepare the Count's dinner.

As soon as she had left, Supercat sprang out of the shadows.

"Tiger power, rargh rargh rargh!" he roared.

He pounced on the Count, knocked him

to the floor and sat on his chest.

"Tell me your evil plan or I will
twang your moustache!"

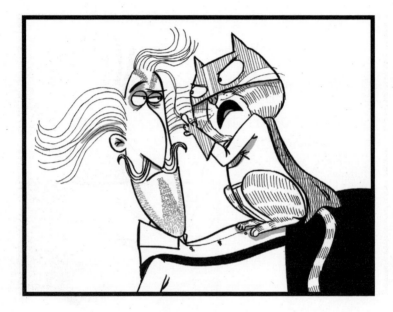

"Twang away!" tittered the Count.
"See if I care."

Supercat gave it a hard yank, but

the moustache came off in his paw
and he fell over backwards. The
Count rocked with laughter.

"Hahaha! You can't stop me now.
It's too late! I'm a whisker away
from creating my own underwater

universe," he said. "Scubatown is just the beginning. I will expand my empire, city by city. Country by country. Soon there will be no one left on dry land. I will have kidnapped everyone, and they will all do my bidding!"

"You're mad," said James.

Count Backwards stood up. His eyelid began to twitch.

"Mad, am I? That's what the Secret Service said. It hurt my feelings, Master Jones, it really did. They left me to rot in jail. I don't like it when people call me mad."

He scowled menacingly at James, tears of anger running down his face, then blew his nose noisily on the hem of Supercat's cape.

"Well now it's my turn to drive *them* mad," the Count sniffed. "I will be King of the Seven Seas and there's nothing they can do to stop me!"

"We'll stop you!" said James and Supercat in unison, standing side by side.

The Count gave them a lop-sided grin.

"Let's do the maths, shall we? One dopey boy plus one daft tabby divided by 5-4-3-2-one Clever Count Backwards and his army of Calculators and brainwashed parents equals... victory for me! As we speak, your mother is cooking my dinner and your father is driving my cabs... Hahaha!"

"What have you done with Mimi?" said James.

"She wasn't meant to be here," scowled the Count. "No children allowed. I hate children. She slipped through the net, so I've put her in maths detention for ten years."

Mimi wasn't James's favourite person, but he wouldn't wish two days of maths detention on his worst enemy, let alone ten years.

"You're truly evil," said James.

The Count sounded genuinely surprised. "Oh," he said. "I thought I was being kind. Personally, I'd regard that as a treat."

He picked up a pot of fish food and sprinkled it into the aquarium, singing to himself.

"*1-2-3-4-5,*

Once I caught a fish alive,

5-4-3-2-1,

I am Mrs Jones's son!"

James could take no more. He grabbed the flute and flung it into the aquarium. The Count watched aghast as it sank down on to the gravel.

"How dare you!" he hissed, grabbing his cutlass off the wall.

"I'm sick of you calling the tune," said James, dodging out of the way. "Look out, Supercat!"

Too late! While Supercat was bending over trying to rub the snot off his cloak, Count Backwards had scooped him up by the waistband with his cutlass and was dangling him

over the aquarium.

"*Ding dong bell, pussy's in the well*," sang the Count. "*Backwards caught him, in he fell*... Fetch my flute, there's a good cat."

Supercat folded his arms.

"No, you fetch it."

By now, Supercat's pants' elastic had stretched so much, his chin was almost touching the water.

"Me? Ooh no," said Count Backwards. "There are electric eels in there. You're in for a nasty shock."

"So are you!" said James, giving the Count's braces a really hard ping. Backwards gave a startled shriek, dropped his cutlass and Supercat plopped into the water. James looked around frantically for some rope to pull him out, but a second later

Supercat appeared again, with the cutlass in his fangs, leaping out of the tank like a salmon.

"Hold on to your hat, it's Supercat!" he whooped, threatening the Count with his own cutlass.

"That's no match for my 1-2-3-4-5 Iron!" said the Count, grabbing a golf club. Swinging it wildly, he knocked the cutlass out of Supercat's paw and chased him over the bed and round the room until he'd backed him up against the aquarium.

"You're bunkered, Supercat," the Count crowed, and with an insane cackle, he swung the club at Supercat's head.

Supercat ducked. There was

129

a terrific **smash** as the tank
shattered.

"You just got a hole in one,"
laughed James, standing on a chair as
salt water flooded into the room, filling
it with squid and sea slugs and crabs.
Ducking just in time to avoid a flying
octopus, Backwards splashed over to
his bedside table and pressed a panic
button.

A couple of Calculators waded into
the room.

"I wish I'd worn my Speedos, Mr
Minus," said Mr Plus, skidding on a
jellyfish.

"I wish you hadn't put that picture
in my head, Mr Plus," said Mr Minus,
picking a starfish off his nose.

More and more Calculators arrived, paddling about in the flooded room with their trousers rolled up, as if they were on a day trip at a crowded beach.

"Seize that boy!" screamed Count Backwards as James grabbed a swordfish and jabbed him with it.

"Grab that mangy cat!"

The Calculators came at them, thick and fast.

"Yow! I've been nipped, Mr Minus," said Mr Plus.

"By a crab, Mr Plus?"

"By a cat, Mr Minus."

Count Backwards stood among the mayhem gazing sadly at his beloved teddy collection, which was bobbing about in the water. Cursing Supercat and James, he screamed at his henchmen. "Get them!"

James and Supercat fought hard, side by side, tooth and claw. But despite

Supercat's best Salami moves and James's quick wit, there were just too many Calculators and in the end they were overwhelmed.

"Take them away!" cried the Count gleefully. "Put them in the scuppers with a hosepipe on them!"

Unable to find a hosepipe, Mr Plus and Mr Minus dragged them out of the castle and drove them back to the tunnel. Pressing the button to open the revolving doors, the Calculators bundled them up the ramp, on to the submarine and locked them in the broom cupboard.

They were trapped.

Chapter Seven

HELLO, SAILOR

It was pitch-black in the broom cupboard. James couldn't see a thing. However, being a cat, Supercat could. He was trying to pick the lock with his claws, but he wasn't having much luck.

"This is a complicated lock. It's claw-proof as well as waterproof. I need a thin bit of metal to twiddle in the hole," he said. "Got a nail file?"

"No," said James. "Ten-year-old boys don't carry nail files as a rule." He sat down on a bucket and triedto think of a plan, but he was struggling.

"Even if we get out of this cupboard, and back through the revolving doors, we can't rescue all the grown-ups by ourselves," he sighed. "Not from under the sea. It's impossible."

Supercat sat down next to him.

"I know what Tigerman would do," he said.

"What?" said James, hoping he'd thought of a brilliant plan.

"He wouldn't give up," said Supercat. "Remember what he said in issue twelve when all the odds were against him?"

James thought back.

"It's impossible for the impossible to be impossible?"

"Believe it, my friend," said Supercat, unhooking the metal handle from a bucket and straightening it. As he jiggled it in the lock, James noticed

his ears were swivelling like pussycat

propellers.

"Beep... beep... beep..." said Supercat.

"What can you hear?" asked James.

"It's sonar!"

"From another submarine?" said James.

Supercat shook his head.

"It's coming from a ship almost directly above us."

James leapt up in excitement.

"Maybe her crew could help us rescue the citizens of Scubatown! The only trouble is, we need to bring this submarine to the surface to contact them."

"It's no trouble at all," said Supercat.

There was a sharp click as he unpicked the lock.

"You did it! Do you really think you can operate this submarine though?" said James.

He'd flown a helicopter, and driven Dad's car, but this was a different kettle of fish.

"Standing on my head," said Supercat, opening the door. "After you, James."

They ran out of the cupboard and searched for the control room.

"Is this it?" said Supercat, bursting into the galley.

"No, that's the kitchen," said James.

Supercat's eyes lit up. He hadn't eaten since breakfast and it was way past lunchtime.

"Can we stay here?" he said, rummaging in the cupboards for food. There seemed to be nothing but pink wafer biscuits (the Count's favourite).

"Come on, there's no time to lose," said James, hurrying Supercat out.

The control room was in the hull. It was large and brightly lit and had two periscopes. In front of the aircraft-style controls were two seats, with a third seat behind.

"Hmm," said James. "It must need three people to operate it."

Supercat looked rather insulted.

"I'm worth two of anybody," he said. "And you're here, so we'll be fine."

He climbed on to the seat. Sitting on chairs always gave him a secret

142

thrill as he wasn't allowed on the furniture at home.

"Right," said James, sitting next to him and studying the controls. "This bit must steer the rudder, and that's the ballast control, which makes the sub go up and down."

"Yes, but how do we get out of this tunnel?" said Supercat.

There was a thick manual under the seat. James flicked through it, talking to himself.

"OK... Press button A to shut and lock door to underwater city."

James pressed it and the revolving

door closed with a satisfying *pshhhlock*.

"I wanted to press it," said Supercat sulkily.

"You can press the next one," said James. Then, reading aloud, "When the green light comes on, press button B to open tunnel exit door." Supercat tapped his claws impatiently as the

traffic lights went from red to amber, then slammed his paw down on one of the buttons. There was a deafening sound like a police siren mixed with a fire-engine bell. Supercat clapped his paws over his ears.

"You hit the collision alarm," said James.

"Pardon?" yelled Supercat.

James turned it off.

"You hit button D instead of button B. Mind that red one too," he said, grabbing Supercat's furry arm and moving it away from danger.

"This is no time for an arm-wrestling competition," said Supercat. "We're on a serious mission."

"You almost fired a torpedo," said James, raising the ramp and closing the escape hatch on the sub. "Tell me when the door behind opens on the exit tunnel."

He turned a dial and threw three switches.

"It's opening..." said Supercat. "The sea's flooding in."

The tunnel filled with water until they were submerged.

"Get ready to reverse out," said James. "You take the rudders, I'll navigate."

"I get to steer? About time too," said Supercat, thrusting the submarine forwards instead of backwards and pranging it on the city door.

"The other way," said James.

"Just testing," said Supercat.

The submarine sped out of the tunnel, did a U-turn and headed across the ocean towards the ship.

James looked through a periscope.
"It's a Navy vessel!" he said.

"I don't care what colour it is," said
Supercat. "Let's take this baby up!"

But as the submarine broke the
surface of the water, they were
greeted by the Navy crew, all
pointing their weapons at them.

"Hello, sailors!" said Supercat
cheerfully. "No need to salute, it's
only us."

"Put your hands above your heads," commanded the captain.

"I haven't got hands, I've got paws," quibbled Supercat.

The captain gave him a hard stare.

"Do as he says," said James nervously.

As they were hauled aboard by two burly seamen, James tried to explain to the captain about Count Backwards's evil plan to kidnap the citizens of the world and hold them captive in his underwater city. It sounded so crazy, the captain decided he couldn't possibly be

150

making it up.

"I've heard some Fishermen's Tales in my time," he said, "but this one takes some beating."

"Will you help us?" said James.

Supercat lifted his mask up and pulled what he hoped was a winning smile.

"Pleeeease?"

The captain took one look at his face and did a double-take.

"You're a cat!"

"I'm not a cat, I'm Supercat!" said Supercat, puffing up his chest.

"Was one of your relatives a

ship's cat by any chance?" asked the captain, looking at him closely. "Only you look just like Mister Tiddles, the tabby who saved me from Red Beard the Pirate."

"My grandfather, Tiddles!" exclaimed Supercat proudly.

"Does he?" said the captain. "Well, we all need to go sometimes... *Oh*, you mean you're grandfather *was* Tiddles?"

He grabbed Supercat's paw and shook it.

"As Tiddles's grandson, I regard you as family," he said. "I'm happy to

help. Action stations, men! Let's

rescue the kidnapped citizens of

Scubatown."

"Thank you, kind sir. Please hop

aboard our submarine," said

Supercat.

The captain looked at the *Dawn Crockabust* doubtfully. It was nothing like any submarine he'd ever seen before. But eventually, after some persuading, he and his crew climbed aboard, watching in terror as Supercat took the controls.

"Never fear, Supercat is here!" he said, narrowly missing a rock as he submerged the submarine.

"Don't worry, Captain. He can do this standing on his head," said James.

"I'd be a lot less frightened if he did it sitting down," said the captain.

To everyone's relief, Supercat got
the submarine down to the sea bed
in one piece and, with James's help,

he docked it safely back in the entry tunnel. The door closed behind them and the water flushed away. As they waited for the traffic lights to change, the captain turned to his troops.

"Are you ready to ambush Count Backwards and save the citizens of Drack Scubatown, lads?" asked the captain.

The troops cheered.

The revolving door to the city spun open.

"Green light!" shouted James.

It was time to do battle.

Chapter Eight

DODGIER THAN DODGEMS

While waiting for his aquarium to be fixed and his teddies to dry out, Count Backwards had decided to play a round of crazy golf out in the square. As his ball stopped short of the windmill, he picked it up

and plopped it down the ninth hole.

"Well played, my Lord," said Mr Plus.

"Excellent shot, Sire!" said Mr Minus.

He was in the middle of his victory dance when, to his horror, hundreds of sailors spilled into the square, led by James and Supercat.

"We're back, Backwards!" quipped Supercat.

With a cowardly shriek, the Count sprinted to the safety of his crystal castle and locked the door behind him.

"You rescue the people, Captain. We'll take care of the Count," said James.

The Navy had already overpowered the Calculators, so while they began to gather the grown-ups and drive them by the coachload back to the submarine, Supercat and James went over to persuade the Count to surrender.

"You can't get away this time!" Supercat shouted through the keyhole. "You're surrounded!"

There was an ominous silence from inside the castle. Then they heard Count Backwards reply in a wheedling, singsong voice:

"The foul little pussy cat went to sea in a submarine-type boat.

He never knew my crystal fort could sink and dive and float..."

161

"I hate it when he sings in riddles. What's he on about now?" said Supercat.

"*That!*" said James, pointing up at the turrets. They were collapsing down, just like the masts on the *Crockabust*. The castle was changing shape before their eyes...

"It's morphing into a submarine too!" said James.

There was a mechanical clunk. James jumped back. The ground beneath them was opening. He watched dumbstruck as the castle lowered itself into a lift shaft that lead to the open sea.

"It's an escape hatch!" said Supercat. "Backwards is getting away!"

They watched in horror as the Count gave them a cheery wave from the top window, sealed safely inside the watertight glass cocoon that was once his castle.

"5-4-3-toodle pip!" he snickered.

As the vessel disappeared, the escape hatch in the floor re-sealed with a clunk.

"Where's he gone?" said Supercat, scanning the glass city wall.

"There'll be an anti-flooding device at the end of the shaft like the one in the exit tunnel," said James. "I expect he's waiting for the green light."

"Tigerman didn't catch villains by waiting for the green light!" growled Supercat, trying in vain to open the escape hatch in the floor. "I'm going after him!"

"How?" said James, hunting for an

emergency button to operate it.

"I'll swim," said Supercat.

Just then, they caught sight of the Count's castle-sub puttering along on the sea bed beneath them.

"It's got a motor," said James. "Even if you swim as fast as a tiger shark, you won't be able to hold your breath long enough to catch him, unless..."

Suddenly, James remembered. One of the market stalls sold diving gear!

"Run and get yourself a wetsuit, a helmet and an oxygen tank," he said.

Supercat was off in a flash, and as the diving stall was deserted, he helped himself to everything he needed. He even found helmets with built-in radio devices, which meant that if both he and James wore one, they could communicate. By the time he'd struggled into the wetsuit and run back in his flippers, James had found an emergency button and had opened the exit hatch ready for him. Supercat prepared to jump into the lift.

"Wait!" said James, snapping his helmet on. "Let's check the radios first. *This is James to Supercat. Do you read me, Supercat?*"

"Read to you?" said Supercat.

"Yes, I read you Tigerman comics at bedtime."

"I meant *can-you-hear-me*?" said James slowly.

Supercat swivelled his ears as best he could in a diving helmet.

"Loud and clear," he said. "A bit too loud if anything. Can I go now?"

James hesitated – he couldn't bear it if anything happened to Supercat. But if he stopped him going, the Count would get away again and who knows what evil plan he would come up with next time?

"OK," James said, with a sigh. He looked out and located the Count, who was cruising through some coral.

"Head for the reef. Good luck!"

"*Merci beaucoup, au revoir!*" said

Supercat, showing off his French as he disappeared down the shaft. The floor closed over him. James waited anxiously for Supercat to appear in the sea on the other side of the glass city wall. The green light was taking ages. He tried to contact him on his radio.

"Are you OK, Supercat?"

There was a worrying silence. James held his breath.

Then Supercat spoke.

"I've got a wedgie," he said. "This wetsuit's a bit snug. Tweaking my pants."

Suddenly, Supercat shot out of the lift shaft into the water. James stopped giggling. It was his job to guide him towards Count Backwards – but where was he?

Just when he thought he'd lost him for good, the castle-sub popped up from behind a giant clam.

"This is James to Supercat. Head north towards the huge seashell."

"Can you narrow it down a bit more?" said Supercat. "There are loads of huge seashells."

"The one with yellow spots," said James.

"Got it!" Supercat flew through the ocean, flapping his flippers like a turbo-charged turtle.

"I'm on your tail, Backwards!" he said triumphantly.

"He can't hear you," said James.

"Then I shall insult him in German," said Supercat. "Backwards, *du ein idiot bist! Dummkopf! Schweinhund!*"

Supercat had almost caught up with his arch-nemesis, when the Count spotted him. Squirting a cloud of ink from the back of his castle-sub, he escaped like a squid.

"Dang!" said Supercat. "Where's he gone? I can't see a thing."

"Swish the ink away," said James. "Keep swishing!"

Supercat whirled his arms wildly until the water went clear. "Right, where is he?"

"There he is! He's behind that bunch of red seaweed straight ahead," said James.

"He can run, but he can't hide!" said Supercat, swimming after him like a furry merman. With one more stroke, he caught up with the Count's castle-sub and grabbed hold of the rudder.

The Count revved the engine angrily, trying to wrench the rudder from Supercat's paws.

"Hold on, Supercat!" shouted James. "You've got him now!"

But just when Supercat was sure he

had him, the rudder came off in his paw. Laughing in his face, the Count puttered off.

"So long, Scubacat!" mocked Backwards. But he didn't laugh for long, as the rudderless vehicle spun

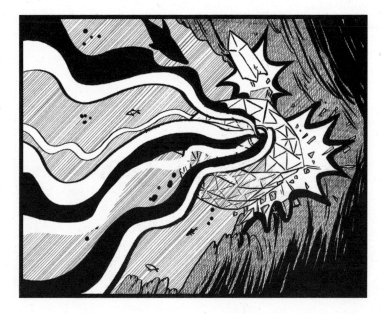

out of control and crashed into a
rock, smashing a gaping hole in its
side. As water gushed into the castle-
sub, an enormous, torpedo-shaped
shadow came looming towards it...
James's heart thumped.

"James to Supercat – Look out!"
he cried. But he couldn't see Supercat
anywhere. Had he swum in after the
Count?

James watched in horror as the
Great White Shark circled the castle-
sub, then swam through the hole in
its side.

There was a long, hideous scream.

"James to Supercat... Are you all right, Supercat?"

Radio silence. James tapped the mouthpiece in his helmet.

"Supercat, do you read me... Supercat?"

But there was no response. James stared miserably out to sea, looking for some sign of his furry friend. Why had he allowed Supercat to put himself in danger? He'd never forgive himself if something had happened to him.

Suddenly his radio crackled.

"This is Supercat. Mission accomplished. The Count is defeated! I am climbing aboard the Navy ship."

James jumped in the air in celebration.

"Woo hoo!" he cried. "You're alive! I'll meet you at the ship!"

James pulled off his helmet and ran to join the queue for the last coach out of Scubatown.

By the time the Navy ship had arrived at the dock and dropped anchor, the ship's doctor had almost finished de-hypnotising all the grown-ups so that they wouldn't remember the awful trauma they'd been through. With a final salute goodbye, James and Supercat pedalled home on the unicycle and were sitting watching the TV when Mum, Dad and Mimi returned an hour later looking none the worse for their adventure.

"Oh, there you are, James," said Mum. "We had a lovely day at the fair. Why did you come home early?"

"I couldn't find you, and it was way past Tiger's teatime," said James.

Unfortunately, the de-hypnotising didn't seem to have worked so well on Mimi.

"It was a *howwible* day!" she said. "We got taken to an underwater city and I was put in maths detention. I saw Tiger there! He was in his pants and vest."

"*Pants and vest?*" scoffed James. "You're nuttier than a coconut shy. Tiger's been asleep on my bed all day. It's all he ever does."

"Then why has he got *seaweed* in his fur?" pouted Mimi.

"It's... cabbage," said James, thinking quickly as he made a speedy exit upstairs. "He's been rolling in the compost heap."

Supercat followed him up the stairs innocently.

"Phew, that was close," said Supercat, closing the bedroom door

behind him. "It was a great day though, wasn't it?"

"One of our finest," said James. "We didn't win the Lucky Dip but it feels like we won the jackpot, beating Count Backwards."

Supercat folded his hero outfit and put it in the back of the wardrobe.

"I don't suppose I'll be needing this any more," he said. "Backwards was dodgier than the dodgems, but surely even *he* couldn't get away from a man-eating shark?"

But stranger things have happened at sea.

EPILOGUE

Deep in the ocean, a shark hiccupped. It had a horrid taste in its mouth. It swam to the surface and spat something out – something half-black, half-white and half-drowned.

"5-4-3-too bad the crash gave me
an Unlucky Dip inside that shark's
stomach," spluttered Count Backwards.

"But I *will* get my revenge on that pesky duo or my name's not Dawson Butcrack!"

Have you read:

SuperCat vs the chip thief

He's a funny, furry, all-action hero!

SuperCat vs the party pooper

The world's funniest all-action cat is back!

Jeanne Willis

If you love Supercat,
you'll love these
AWESOME ANIMAL
adventures
from **Jeanne Willis:**

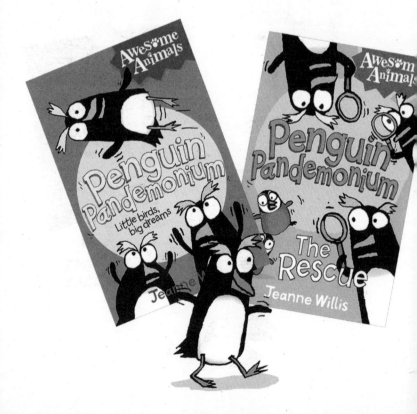

Get your **PAWS** on these other great books from **HARPERCOLLINS:**

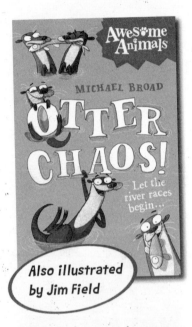

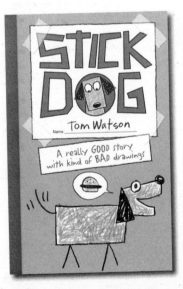